PU

Diary of an Alien

When he was eight years old, the thing Noel Ford enjoyed most at school was telling stories. He would stand up in front of the class and make up the stories as he went along, illustrating them on the blackboard. He never knew what was going to happen – he was just as keen as everyone else to find out!

Whenever the other children discussed what they wanted to be when they grew up – usually nurses and engine drivers – Noel used to think how terrific it would be if he could get a job telling stories and drawing funny pictures. That's what he does now, drawing cartoons for magazines and newspapers and writing and illustrating books like this. And he was right – it is really terrific!

He has done other things too. He used to play lead guitar in a band and once worked in a school science lab (he left that job after nearly blowing the place up).

These days Noel lives in a quiet Leicestershire village with his wife, his daughter and Tuppence and Penny, two demented golden retrievers. He finds it safer to leave anything dangerous to the characters in his books and cartoons.

DIARY OF AN ALIEN

The journal of a young extraterrestrial
stranded on the planet Earth.
(It was all his mum's fault.)

Earth-English Language Edition
written and illustrated by
Noel Ford

Note:
This special edition has been published in
the ancient style known to primitive
Earthlings as 'a book'.

PUFFIN BOOKS

PUFFIN BOOKS

Published by the Penguin Group
Penguin Books Ltd, 27 Wrights Lane, London W8 5TZ, England
Penguin Books USA Inc., 375 Hudson Street, New York, New York 10014, USA
Penguin Books Australia Ltd, Ringwood, Victoria, Australia
Penguin Books Canada Ltd, 10 Alcorn Avenue, Toronto, Ontario, Canada M4V 3B2
Penguin Books (NZ) Ltd, 182–190 Wairau Road, Auckland 10, New Zealand

Penguin Books Ltd, Registered Offices: Harmondsworth, Middlesex, England

First published by Viking 1994
Published in Puffin Books 1996
1 3 5 7 9 10 8 6 4 2

Made and printed in England by Clays Ltd, St Ives plc

DAY 1

Some holiday this has turned out to be! Left alone in this crummy space caravanette orbiting an unexplored planet, while Mum and Dad are off chasing hydrogen atoms.

What's more, this lump of space junk is parked in what Dad calls a Geo-Sin-Kronic orbit (or something like that), which means it is always over the same place on the planet's surface and the view from my window is always the same. I'm really fed up!

It's all Mum's fault. Well, let's be fair, partly Dad's fault too, but it was Mum's idea in the first place.

'Let's go somewhere *different* for our holiday this year,' she said. 'Let's explore the outer planets. They say there are some lovely old-fashioned worlds out there, off the beaten track. We could go self-catering – rent a caravanette from Uncle Zog. He'd knock something off for *family*.'

Well, it sounded a lot better (at the

7

time) than our annual jaunt to the **BUGLIN'S HAPPY HOLIDAY SATELLITE.** (*'There are no STRANGERS at BUGLIN'S, only FRIENDLY EXOTIC SPECIES you haven't met.'*...Yuk!)

Dad took some persuading – he always won the Knobbly Tentacles competition at Buglin's – but he came around to Mum's way of thinking when she threatened to turn on the tears. *His* tears!

So off we trooped to **ZOG'S RENT-A-RELIC USED SPACE VEHICLE HIRE.**

OPEN-AIR BARBECUE – MAKE SURE YOU HAVE AN ATMOSPHERE

ANTI-THEFT SENSOR – NOT WORKING

LUCKY MASCOT – ALSO NOT WORKING

FOG LIGHTS FOR USE IN STAR CLOUDS

FUNNY SAUCER-SHAPED THINGY

METEORITE-SHOWER
DEFLECTION GEAR

HYPERDRIVE TURBO-
BOOSTER – 0–60 IN
0.000017695 NANO-
SECONDS WITH
THE SOLAR WIND
BEHIND YOU

OUTBOARD
HYDROGEN
ENGINE

MY ROOM

HAPPY
WANDERER
Mk III

HOLES FOR FIXING UP
AWNING ON CAMPSITES

CAT-FLAP

TOWING BRACKET

GOODNESS KNOWS
WHAT THIS IS FOR

Mum was dead right
about Uncle Zog. He did knock
something off for *'family'*. He
knocked off this space caravanette.

Nicked it the day before we went to see him and then hired it out to us. We were only half a light year into our journey when Dad saw the flashing blue lights in his rear-view telescreen.

Next, an official voice came over our crackly communication system:

PULL OVER. **ORBITAL POLICE**. WE
HAVE REASON TO BELIEVE YOU ARE
IN POSSESSION OF A **MARK 3** *HAPPY
WANDERER* SPACE CARAVANETTE
REPORTED STOLEN FROM OUTSIDE
**SIX-EYED WALLY'S AMUSEMENT
ARCADE**.

Dad panicked. He jumped up and ran around the cabin pulling his hair out in orange and purple chunks, using words I didn't understand.

Except for *Uncle Zog*, that is. He used *those* two words quite a few times.

In his panic (Dad claims), he pressed the **HYPERDRIVE** button instead of the **STOP** button.

WHOOOOOOMPH!

In less time than it takes a Dorkian Fraggle-Warbler to trongle its floop, we were zipped off, thousands of light years further than we intended. Way past the outer planets. Beyond the outer-outer planets. All the way to this primitive lump of rock I can see outside my window. With every molecule of our fuel used up.

Dad asked the computer for our position and it said:

DESPERATE

Then it apologized for its feeble electronic joke and said:

**PLANET EARTH.
NO FURTHER INFORMATION
AVAILABLE AT THIS
PARTICULAR MOMENT IN
SPACE-TIME.**

EARTH! WHAT A STUPID
NAME
FOR A PLANET MOSTLY
COVERED
WITH WATER!

THIS MAP WAS COMPILED WITH THE HAPPY WANDERER MARK 3
COMPUTER, WHICH, THOUGH FAIRLY INTELLIGENT IN SOME
RESPECTS, IS ABSOLUTELY HOPELESS AT GEOGRAPHY.

So here we are, circling this feeble planet with an empty fuel tank. And here's the best part. This space caravanette is so old that it has *hydrogen* engines. Yes, don't laugh, *hydrogen*.

The good news is that, just below us, in the Earth's atmosphere, there are lots of hydrogen atoms. The bad news is, we need to move the *caravanette* to get *them* but we need *them* in order to move the *caravanette*.

That's why Mum and Dad have left me here to go off in the space dinghy to collect hydrogen atoms by hand.

It's going to take a long time. Space isn't entirely empty, you know. In every cubic centimetre there is one hydrogen atom. We only need three or four zillion zillion of them.

Equipment you need to collect hydrogen atoms by hand

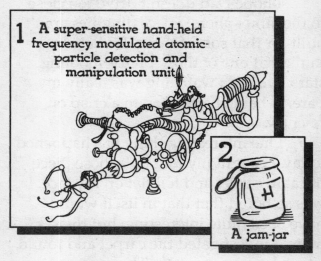

1 A super-sensitive hand-held frequency modulated atomic-particle detection and manipulation unit

2 A jam-jar

I think I shall go to sleep now.
Logging this diary into my Memory Implant is making my brains ache. All three of them.

I hope to have something more encouraging to report tomorrow, but I doubt it.

DAY 2

I was right. I'm still here and Mum and Dad are still out there.

I hope Dad doesn't drive too close to the atmosphere. Space dinghies aren't built for that sort of thing. I'd hate to think that one of those pretty shooting stars I've been watching was really my parents being barbecued to a crisp on re-entry.

One interesting thing has happened today. I caught my foot on a loose piece of cabin carpet and fell flat on my face. I was so bored that that in itself would have been quite interesting, but there's more. I investigated the carpet and found a trapdoor underneath. There was a sign:

```
FOR
EMERGENCY
USE ONLY
OPEN WITH
SPECIAL KEY
```

I have searched for the key, but I can't find it. There is a box on the wall with a broken glass front and a sign saying:

IN EMERGENCY BREAK GLASS

There is a hook inside. The hook is empty. As the old proverb says, *Only a fool squints at a wangle tree on Thursdays.**

> *English edition translator's note: This proverb loses a little in the translation.

DAY 3

I've found the key! The answer was staring me in the eye (the yellow one) all the time.

I was playing a boring game on the computer: **ATTACK OF THE TWO-LEGGED CREATURE FROM OUTER SPACE** – well, it was that or listen, for the zillionth time, to **SING ALONG WITH THE MAGNUS MAJOR METEORITE-MINERS' MALE**

VOICE CHOIR (50 COSMIC FAVOURITES),
the caravanette's one and only music
capsule. Suddenly the program crashed,
and up on the screen came the log-book
of the caravanette's real owner.

The first few entries were *really*
interesting. Ha! – I *don't* think – Ha!

**WENT TO HAPPY
WANDERER CARAVANETTE CLUB
MEETING ON POGRON MINOR.**

And:

**EXCITING DAY! ELECTED HAPPY
WANDERER CLUB HYGIENE
OFFICER.**

I was about to switch off when up
came:

**HAD NOSEBLEED ON WAY TO
HAPPY WANDERER RALLY.
DROPPED EMERGENCY KEY
DOWN BACK OF NECK TO
STOP IT. PUT EMERGENCY
KEY IN FIRST-AID KIT.**

And that is where I found it.

Now that I have it, I'm not sure that I should use it. After all, it does say **FOR EMERGENCY USE ONLY.**

Should I? I think I'll sleep on it.

DAY 4

The **EMERGENCY** has arrived. Dad called on the com-link to tell me that the dinghy has broken down. He asked me to see if the computer had any suggestions.

It grumbled about being interrupted in the middle of a game of twenty-five dimensional patience and then told me:

**ELECTRONIC DATA
SWEEP OF PLANET EARTH
REVEALS PRIMITIVE
CIVILIZATION WHICH HAS
EVOLVED SOMETHING
CALLED THE NATIONAL
BREAKDOWN SERVICE.
UNFORTUNATELY YOU HAVE
TO BE A MEMBER AND**

**WE'RE A BIT OUT
OF THEIR AREA.
THERE IS ALSO SID'S
24-HOUR REPAIRS,
BUT 24 HOURS SEEMS
A LONG TIME TO HAVE
TO WAIT. SORRY.**

I have told Dad and he says not to worry, he thinks he can fix it himself.

Not worry? Ha! I remember the time Dad '*fixed*' our dishwasher. Our best dinner-service is still in orbit!

Flying saucer spotted circling moon on day Dad fixed the dishwasher

Note: Later, reports came in of flying cups, plates, soup dishes...

So I decided to use the key. I opened the trapdoor and lowered myself into a narrow tube. There was another trapdoor at the bottom, which sprang open as soon as my lower tentacles touched it. I found myself in a small spherical room.

The whole thing was padded, apart from a screen and a control panel. There was more to this caravanette than I'd thought!

At this point, a red button on the control panel began to flash. The screen lit up with the message:

DO NOT
PRESS THIS BUTTON
UNLESS YOU ARE
REALLY
SERIOUS

Well, what would you have done?

As I pressed the button, the message changed:

ESCAPE CAPSULE
ACTIVATED
RELEASE FROM MAIN
VEHICLE IN R-MINUS

10 ...

9 ... 8 ... 7 ... 6 ...

As I record these (possibly final) thoughts, I am entering Earth's atmosphere in the escape capsule of a rickety old rust-bucket of a space cara-vanette. I am not entirely convinced it is up to the task.

This journal will be continued *if* my re-entry is successful.

HOW TO CHECK IF YOUR RE-ENTRY HAS BEEN SUCCESSFUL

After capsule has entered atmosphere, do the following:

1 Sing a song

2 Do a dance

3 Try to remember what you were doing last week

If you can do all of these things, your re-entry has been SUCCESSFUL ✓

If you can't do ANY of these things it is probably because a SMOULDERING PILE OF ASH can't sing, dance or remember what it was doing last week. In which case, your re-entry has been UNSUCCESSFUL ✗

DAY 5

Have you ever done something and then asked yourself, 'What came over me? Why did I have to go and do that?'?

Why, for instance, did I have to tell the truth when Aunt Megabyte asked me if I agreed that her new head-transplant made her look 130 years younger?

Why, for instance, did I have to press a red button which said DO NOT PRESS THIS BUTTON UNLESS YOU ARE REALLY SERIOUS?

As you have realized, since I am still here, I did land safely. That was this morning though, and since then things haven't been so good.

Now seems like a good time to bring things up to date – there isn't a lot else I can do, locked up in this little cage.

My trip down to Earth was uneventful, apart from a near-collision with a *Concorde*.

Dad told me before we embarked on this holiday that places beyond the inner planets would probably be a little old-fashioned.

Wrong!

A planet with flying machines like this *Concorde*, old-fashioned? Never!

Brain-bogglingly primitive is closer to the mark. I ask you – *jet engines*, for goodness' sake.

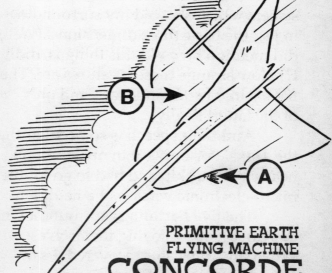

PRIMITIVE EARTH
FLYING MACHINE
CONCORDE

Because this machine uses primitive jet engines (A), it has to keep moving to stay in the air. No stopping for repairs or sightseeing! Note that, although it has rather nice open-air decks (B), the passengers prefer to stay indoors in the tiny, cramped cabin.

Anyway – surprise, surprise – the escape capsule's anti-collision system worked and I missed *Concorde* with a good three millimetres to spare.

And – another surprise – when I landed, the capsule's defence shields were working, making it invisible to the Earth inhabitants around me.

I examined those inhabitants on the screen, which showed my surroundings in just the basic three dimensions. (Well, I did mention how old this thing is, didn't I?) How strange these creatures are. They have jointed *arms* and *legs* – and only *two* of the latter! Really!

And their speech is so peculiar that the Translator Implant in my left brain nearly blew a chip and had to go for the micro-electronic version of a lie-down.

The five Earthlings surrounding me appeared to be enjoying themselves. When my Translator recovered, I saw why. A sign in the distance said:

I was in a zoo! That explained the wire mesh which I could see on the screen. The Earthlings were watching the antics of the animals behind the wire.

These animals also had just two arms and legs each and looked even stranger than the Earthlings. They seemed to be very excited, jumping up and down and waving their arms, pointing at the Earthlings and exposing their teeth in huge grins.

Thank goodness for that wire. I wouldn't like to meet one of those on a dark night. Those teeth looked sharp.

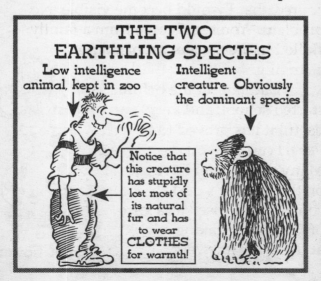

THE TWO EARTHLING SPECIES

Low intelligence animal, kept in zoo

Intelligent creature. Obviously the dominant species

Notice that this creature has stupidly lost most of its natural fur and has to wear CLOTHES for warmth!

At this point, I remembered my present circumstances were not all that wonderful.

I was stuck on an alien planet with no idea of how I was going to rejoin Mum and Dad.

I switched the screen off and set all three brains to work on the problem.

After a while I came to a decision. I would leave the capsule and set off in search of a radio device. Even a planet as primitive as this one must have discovered radio waves by now.

Leaving the capsule meant, of course, that I would become visible. No problem. You see, I come from a family skilled in the ancient art of shape-changing.

Dad taught me before I started school, and very useful it has proved to be *there*, I can tell you. Many's the time I have sat on the teacher's desk-console, disguised as a vase of flowers, sneaking a look at the exam answers.

Me, as a vase of flowers

The decision made, I acted, before I had time to change any of my minds. Switching on the screen I stared at the Earthlings and…*C.H..A...N....G.....E......D.......*

A quick check:

Two arms…yes.

Two legs…yes.

I was ready. I left the capsule. There was a *WHOOSH!* and I realized that the idiot owner of the caravanette had programmed the capsule to make return trips! Oh well.

Me again, shape-changed into an Earthling (I think I'd rather be a vase of flowers)

Now there were six Earthlings – five real ones plus me. The five real ones didn't notice me. They were too busy climbing up the ropes – provided, I presumed, to enable them to see the animals better.

I couldn't help but feel that there was something different about the Earthlings now that I could see them properly. Before I could put my tentacle on it, though, the animals behind the wire went wild, jabbering, screaming and pointing.

I wasn't too worried. The wire protected me.

Then I noticed a funny thing about the wire. Now that I was outside the capsule I could see that it stretched all around the five Earthlings and myself. I realized that this was a safari-park type of zoo, where the animals roam freely and the spectators watch from within

NORMAL ZOO   THIS ZOO

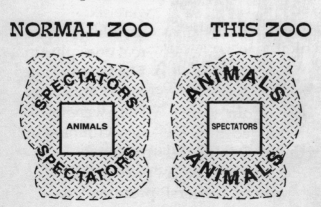

safe enclosures.

I walked around, trying to find the exit. I couldn't find it!

Never mind, I thought. I'll wait for the other Earthlings to leave, and follow them.

Then it happened. The animals were still going crazy on the other side of the wire and suddenly one of them came right up to the wire and pointed something at me.

PHUT!

I felt a sharp pain in my side, looked down and saw a dart poking out of my fur.

I woke up a little while ago in this cage. I think it must be a primitive sort of hospital ward. The Earthlings must have brought me here to treat my wound.

I hope that they haven't destroyed the animal that shot me. It wasn't *its* fault that someone was careless enough to leave a tranquillizer gun lying around where it could get its hand on it.

DAY 6
morning

I have made an interesting discovery. It's a bit embarrassing really.

The people I thought were the *Earthlings* are the *animals*. Chimps, they are called.

And – you've guessed it – what I took to be the *animals* are the *Earthlings*.

I realized my mistake when two *real* Earthlings came into my room this morning.

It was the clothes that had fooled me.

Throughout the civilized galaxy, as you know, only the lower animals wear clothes. Only the lower animals are stupid enough to lose all their natural fur and then have to invent clothes to replace it.

On Earth, something has gone wrong. The lower (clothed) animals are in charge and the higher (furry) life-forms, like the chimps, allow it.

Anyway, these two Earthlings came up to my cage and stared at me. They each wore a badge, one with ERIC written on it, the other GEORGE.

With horror, I recognized GEORGE.

TWO 'GENUINE' EARTHLINGS
These creatures appear to have such poor memories that they have to wear labels to remind them who they are. Amazingly, it is possible that they have only ONE brain!

He was the one who had shot me.

They began talking, but I was too shocked to listen properly.

Luckily, my Memory Implant recorded everything.

MEMORY IMPLANT RETRIEVAL:

GALDATE : 344/67/3388/876

GALTIME: 567/782

INTERCOSMIC CO-ORDINATES:

X98245.562

Y346639.3002

K77.9935524301

LOCAL WEATHER: QUITE NICE FOR TIME
OF YEAR, BUT IT LOOKS A BIT LIKE RAIN.

<ERIC>

It's a funny business, this, George.
There were definitely only five chimps in
there when I fed them. I didn't believe that
bloke when he started raving about another
one appearing in front of his eyes.

<GEORGE>

He was right, though. We didn't even
have to count them. The moment we
looked in the cage and saw this one with
the bright green fur, we knew something
was wrong.

[PAUSE]

Yes, you've guessed. That's what

looked different when I left the capsule. When I copied those chimps from the picture on the screen, I didn't know that the colour was on the blink!

[CONTINUE]
<ERIC>
Lucky you had the dart-gun handy and we got the thing out of the cage before too many people saw it. The newspapers have been phoning all morning, but the boss said to say nothing and to keep it here in the animal hospital until she gets back.

<GEORGE>
Yeah. She would be away when this happened. I'm surprised she believed you when you phoned her.

<ERIC>
She didn't at first. She said I must be drunk, and you know I haven't touched a drop for nearly six months – not since the day I fell in the penguin pool. Remember? I opened my mouth to yell for help and that old lady threw me a sardine!

<GEORGE>
Yeah. And everyone clapped when you caught it. Ha! Ha! Haaaaaaaaaaaaaaa!
[PAUSE]

George began to shake violently, doubling up and making the weird *haaa*-ing sound, as if he were choking.

I feared the onslaught of a terrible illness. Perhaps I had brought a virus to Earth, harmless to me but deadly to Earthlings.

What if the disease spread? What if everyone on the planet was wiped out because of little *me*?

Like most lads, I've done some pretty awful things in my time. I've pulled the leg off a one-legged hoppabug and I've replaced the elastic in my best friend's sister's space-suit bottoms with a stretch-snake.

But I've never killed off the entire population of a medium-sized planet before.

I was getting quite worried, when the truth dawned. George wasn't *dying*.

This was the way that humans *laugh*!
Phew!

[CONTINUE]
<ERIC>
Cut it out, George. Let's feed this thing and get out. The boss can sort everything out when she gets back this afternoon.
[END]

With this, Eric pushed something through the bars of my cage and the two Earthlings left.

I wasn't hungry – I had only eaten ten days ago – but, out of curiosity, I examined the thing Eric had dropped into my cage.

It was yellow and bent, tapering at each end.

In an odd sort of way it looked familiar, so I consulted the Encyclopaedia Implant in my central brain.

ENCYCLOPAEDIA GALAXIA
DIRECT BRAIN-IMPLANT EDITION
(THIS VERSION TO FIT ALL BRAIN SIZES UP TO **VERY SMALL**)

REFERENCE: 49.236[5]
GLUMWICH *Glum-Wich* N. CROSS REFERENCE/TRANSLATOR IMPLANT: Known on planet *Earth* as a **BOOMERANG** *Boo-Mer-Ang*.

A primitive throwing weapon common to early civilizations throughout the known galaxy. The weapon is most regularly associated with tribes of a pessimistic disposition, since it is specifically designed to return to the thrower when it misses its intended target.

It is interesting to note that those tribes failing to master the art of throwing (and catching) the glumwich tended to die out early on in their development (see illustration below).

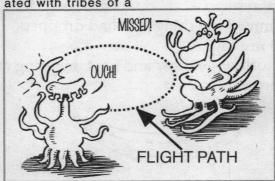

MISSED!

OUCH!

FLIGHT PATH

A native of the planet Oz tries unsuccessfully to hit a quangaroo with his glumwich.

36

Yes! There it was.

Now, why would Eric give me a boomerang? You can't eat a weapon. There can be only one answer.

Eric is one of us! One of our shape-changing secret agents sent out to explore alien planets.

What a stroke of luck he is here, disguised as a zoo-keeper. He has obviously guessed who I really am. Now everything will be all right.

DAY 6
afternoon

I have had several visitors.

The first was another Earthling, shorter than Eric and George and with longer hair. Different shape, too, sticking *out* where the other two *didn't* and *in* where they *did*.

Judging from the fear in their voices earlier, when they mentioned 'she', the boss, I am assuming that Eric and George are males. In which case, the *new* Earthling must be female.

FEMALE   MALE

Note that sticking-out bits
are in opposite places.

She wore a garment over her upper
body and, instead of a badge, her name
was written right across it:

SAVE-THE-WHALES brought in
another creature, popped it in one of the
other cages, and left.

This creature, another higher life-form (it still had its own feathers and wasn't wearing any clothes), looked very unhappy.

No wonder this poor creature looks unhappy. It is homesick for its natural habitat where it used to play with its friends in the deep snow. (It has obviously evolved those large feet for this purpose.)

It tried to talk to me, but it just repeated the same word, over and over again.

'QUACK...QUACK...QUACK...'

My Translator Implant must have been on the blink again because the translation came out as, 'QUACK...QUACK...QUACK...'

I had an idea. Perhaps the poor creature was pining for one of its own kind. I had to help the poor thing, so I shape-changed quickly, taking care to copy the creature exactly.

No sooner had I changed than the door opened and in came Eric and George. With them was another of the curvy-shaped Earthlings. I guessed she was 'the boss'.

I was right. This is what my Memory Implant recorded:

MEMORY IMPLANT RETRIEVAL:

GALDATE : 344/67/3388/876

GALTIME: 567/793

INTERCOSMIC CO-ORDINATES:

X98245.562

Y346639.3002

K77.9935524301

LOCAL WEATHER: THE RAIN IS HOLDING OFF, BUT IT'S REALLY NOT VERY NICE FOR GOING OUT.

\<BOSS\>
All right, then. Show me this green chimpanzee.

\<ERIC\>
Right over here, boss. In this…

\<GEORGE\>
Urk!

<ERIC>
Ah…er…

<BOSS>
Is this some kind of joke?

<GEORGE>
Errr…

<BOSS>
I realize, gentlemen, that I have only been a zoologist for thirty years and that I still have a lot to learn about animals.

However – and here I bow to your superior knowledge – to me, this creature looks remarkably
like
a
DUCK!
In fact, it looks like the twin sister of the other DUCK, over there!

<GEORGE>
Honest, boss, there was a green chimp in there this morning. Eric gave it a banana. It's still there, look. It didn't eat it, the little monkey!

<BOSS>
But it isn't a little MONKEY, is it?
It's a DUCK!
[STOP]

Here, Eric put his face up to my cage and stared at me.

Clever Eric. He must have hypnotized the others into believing that my *boomerang* is an edible object called a *banana*.

While he was so close up, I took the chance of whispering to him.

Unfortunately it came out as, 'QUACK...QUACK...QUACK...' so I just gave him a big wink.

Immediately, his face twisted into a funny shape (a difficult thing to do when you are disguised as an Earthling and your face is already a funny shape), and he made a noise that I have only heard once before in my life, when Dad sat on a ten-pronged needle-nettle.

DAD
(somewhere up there)

TEN-PRONGED
NEEDLE-
NETTLE

Obviously a secret sig-nal. He had understood my sign. Now we both knew that we both knew who we both were.

If you see what I mean.

Eric staggered back from the cage (wonderful acting) and left the room, saying he wasn't feeling well and he was going home.

So, that must be the plan.

I am to escape, using the *banana* if force is necessary, and meet him at his home.

Pity he hasn't told me his address.

DAY 6
evening

Escape! As soon as the Earthlings left, I shape-changed, copying the boss from memory.

I forgot that the boss was bigger than the cage I was in, so my head is still sore where it crashed through the top. Ah, well – it saved me having to solve the problem of how to break out of the cage.

I left the room and entered a corridor, just as SAVE-THE-WHALES came through the door at the far end.

CLANG!

She dropped the bucket she was carrying and stared at me. It turned out that she had just been talking to the boss outside and was somewhat surprised to meet her *inside.*

Quick as a flash, my nimble brains came up with a suitable explanation. I smiled at SAVE-THE-WHALES and said…

'QUACK!'

My translator was playing up again. I lifted one of my unfamiliar arms and gave my head a whack.

'Boss? Are you all right?' SAVE-THE-WHALES asked.

Recovering my composure, I assured her that I was as fit as a furzlegunk in a grummet shop, and walked out. She didn't look too well her-self, I thought.

Outside, I decided that another shape-change was necessary – I couldn't risk being recognized again. I looked for somewhere convenient to change.

Just the place, I thought, reading the sign. The small building had two

PUBLIC CONVENIENCE

doors, each with a picture of an Earthling. One wearing trousers, the other a skirt.

I understood at once that one door was for Earthlings wearing trousers and the other was for Earthlings wearing skirts. I'm not a dunce, you know!

I was wearing a skirt, so I went in through that door. Inside were more doors and, opening one, I found myself in a tiny cubicle containing a peculiar chair with a hole in the middle. Closing the door, I sat down.

Perhaps these Earthlings aren't quite as stupid as I thought. These small buildings are evidently provided for the CONVENIENCE of the PUBLIC. They are places where people can get away from the crowds and sit quietly alone, meditating on their problems.

EARTH MEDITATION ROOM

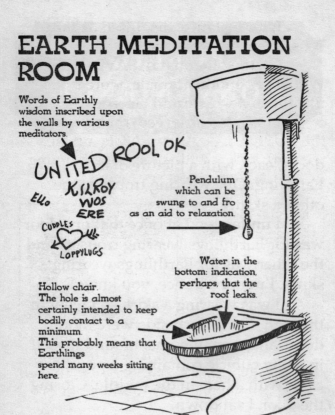

Words of Earthly wisdom inscribed upon the walls by various meditators.

UNITED ROOL OK

ELLO

KILROY
WOS
ERE

CODDLES

LOPPYLUGS

Pendulum which can be swung to and fro as an aid to relaxation.

Water in the bottom: indication, perhaps, that the roof leaks.

Hollow chair. The hole is almost certainly intended to keep bodily contact to a minimum. This probably means that Earthlings spend many weeks sitting here.

I meditated on mine.

Why, I puzzled, should people wearing skirts have to meditate in a different place to those wearing trousers? If the building had different doors for males and females, I could understand it. This, however, is not the case.

I, for instance, disguised as the boss, a female, wore a skirt.

On the other hand, SAVE-THE-WHALES, another female, wore trousers, like the males, Eric and George.

I had also observed, on my way to the PUBLIC CONVENIENCE, a male wearing a skirt with a handbag hanging down the front. Most confusing.

I could have meditated for a long time on this problem, but my eye, the red one, spotted something on the floor of my cubicle. Sheets of paper covered in printing and pictures. In large print on the first sheet were the words **THE DAILY MESSENGER.**

Great. By copying various bits of the Earthlings in **THE DAILY MESSENGER**'s pictures, I could shape-change into someone completely inconspicuous.

Here is what I have chosen:

Stunning new production of *Swan Lake* by the Duckpond Ballet Company

by
The Messenger's Arts Correspondent

This week, the Duckpond Ballet Company, under the direction of its founder, Dame Mildred Duckpond, opened their stunning new blah blah Swan Lake. Blaah blaaaa blah blah blah blaaaah blah blah breathtaking blah blah blah blah blaaah blaah. **THRILLING** Blah blah bl so thrilling I nearly woke up. Blah blah blah blaaahh blah blaaah blah blah blah blah blaah blaaah. **MELTING** Blah blah blah choc-ice began melting blah blaaaah blah blaah blaaaah blah blah blah bl blaan blaaah blaaah blah blaaaah blaaah blah blaaaaaah. **DROPPED** Blah blah blah blah blah blah such a pity when the silly twerp dropped her into the orchestra pit. Blah blah blah.

If you could
EAT LIKE A NORSE
come to
THE VIKING RESTAURANT

EASY WIN FOR MAULERS IN UNEVENTFUL FRIENDLY

by
The Messenger's ~~War~~ Sports Correspondent

Maulers Rugby FC romped home to an easy 298 points to nil win in their friendly game against a scratch team from the Drab Street Brownie Pack. The brownies were a last minute substitute for the Gasworks Rugby FC whose members suddenly discovered that they had urgent business abroad when they heard that they were due to play the Maulers. **BORING** Despite occasional flashes of inspiration from Maulers' scrum-half, Fairyfeet Flanhagan, the game was a boring affair, with only three broken arms, a fractured skull and two dislocated shoulder-blades in the first half blaaaah blah blah blaaaah blah blaah blah blah blaaah blaaaah blah b l a a a a h blaaah blah bblaah and swallowed his false teeth blaaaah blah blaah blah blaaaah blah blaah blah blah blaa and the referee's condition is described as satisfactory. blah blaaaah.

Me, in my inconspicuous disguise

So here I am, shape-changed again. This time I shall be completely anonymous and will attract no special attention. I shall sleep now and, in the morning, venture forth from the peace and security of the PUBLIC CONVENIENCE.

DAY 7
morning and afternoon

I must not set fire to the science lab
I must not set fire to the science lab
I must not...

Oops! Sorry about that. I'll explain later. It's been a funny day.

I haven't found Eric's house yet – haven't had a chance to look! Here's what has happened so far...

Leaving the PUBLIC CONVENIENCE, I noticed that the sun (Earth only has one) was well up in the sky.

I had overslept.

I made my way out of the zoo, getting a few odd glances on the way. For a moment I was worried that perhaps my disguise

THE SUN
EARTH ONLY HAS ONE SUN. LOOKS LONELY, DOESN'T IT?

51

wasn't as inconspicuous as I had hoped. I needn't have worried – the first three people I met in the street were dressed exactly like me. The only difference was *they* were carrying red buckets.

The street, I noticed, was lined with Earthlings, and down the middle of the roadway brightly decorated vehicles carrying brightly decorated Earthlings moved slowly along on old-fashioned wheels.

THE WHEEL
SIMILAR TO THE
SUN ONLY NOT
QUITE AS OLD

There was a lot of noise and everyone was making those funny laughing sounds. I had a moment of doubt.

Perhaps I had been wrong about George.

Had he really been ill?

Was I witnessing the outbreak of the fatal epidemic?

No. I saw the banner, and understood:

CARNIVAL DAY

So the Earthlings have carnivals, too!

One of the vehicles had a sign saying, MAULERS RUGGER CLUB, and it was carrying more people dressed like me. They, too, had buckets, and were using them to catch small metal discs thrown by the crowd.

'Here! What are you doing?' A large hand gripped my shoulder.

What? Caught already? How had I slipped up?

I turned to face the owner of the hand. It was one of the MAULERS.

'You can't collect money without a bucket, you berk,' he yelled, and thrust one of the red buckets into my hand. I took it, gratefully, and made off down the street.

Before long, my bucket was half full of the metal discs. *Money!* Fancy that –

they still use *money* on Earth. This was good news. I might need to buy things and my **JUNIOR INTERGALACTIC EXCESS CREDIT CARD** wasn't going to be much use here, was it?

I could use this money in the bucket, though.

I slipped away down a side-street, turned a corner and...

...stopped.

Two huge Earthlings blocked my path. I thought they were quite good-

looking, for Earthlings. Their yellow
fangs were especially attractive and,
unlike anyone else I had met here, they
each had three eyes, like normal folk.

Then I realized they were wearing
masks. Carnival masks.

'Hand over the bucket,' one of
them said. The other one held out
his hand and I noticed he had
MOTHER written on his arm,
in blue letters.

Strange. He didn't look like a
female, even with the pretty mask.

'The bucket!' the first Earthling
repeated.

I sized up the situation instantly.
These were two carnival officials whose
job was to gather the money collected in

the buckets. But I needed this money. I explained that I hadn't finished collecting and that he and his *MOTHER* should come back later.

MOTHER took a step closer and said, 'Listen, slimeface, how do you fancy a knuckle sandwich?'

Wow! These Earth females! We'd only just met and here she was, chatting me up and asking me out for a meal.

Before I could explain that I had only eaten less than two weeks ago and that she wasn't my type, the other one turned nasty and tried to snatch my bucket.

So, they wanted to play rough!

'Stay where you are,' I growled, 'or you'll get a taste of *this*.' I whipped out the boomerang.

MOTHER said, 'Thanks,' took the boomerang from me, removed it from its yellow case, and bit the end off.

Is it possible that I have been misinformed about boomerangs?

No time to worry about that. Gripping my bucket tightly, I ran off at top speed, determined to shape-change into a copy of the first Earthling I met.

It was a young female – a *girl*. She was standing just around the corner and, oddly, she smiled and gave a little wave as though she knew me. I memorized her as I ran past and was already beginning to change before I rounded the next corner.

I stopped, feeling exhausted, leaned against a wall and slid down to the ground. I was the double of the girl – long fair hair, blue dress, shoulder-bag – but changing had taken all my energy.

There was no one in sight. I had lost the carnival officials. I just had time to transfer the money into my shoulder-bag before falling asleep.

I dreamed I was back home, happily playing tentacleball with my mates.

Less happy things were happening while I slept, though, as my ever-alert Memory Implant recorded:

MEMORY IMPLANT RETRIEVAL:

GALDATE: 344/67/3388/879

GALTIME: 567/951

INTERCOSMIC CO-ORDINATES:

X98245.567

Y346639.3014

K77.9935524301

LOCAL WEATHER: GETTING A BIT STICKY.

<VOICE 1>
Here she is, Timmings. Lucky the school caretaker spotted her and tipped us off. Look at her, fast asleep. You'd think butter wouldn't melt in her mouth.

<VOICE 2>
Yes, headmaster. At least the little troublemaker's only sneaking off today and

not vandalizing the school.

Yes, well, come on, Timmings. Wake her up and get her back. She may not like having to come in to school on Carnival Day, but she should have thought of that before she burned the science lab down.
[STOP]

So, here I am, sitting in a classroom, writing *I must not set fire to the science lab* five thousand times.

I shall soon be finished. I am using both hands (and both feet when Mr Timmings, the teacher, isn't looking).

No problem. My left brain can handle that while my central one brings this journal up to date...
I must not set fire to the science lab
I must not set fire to the science lab
There. Finished. Now I can get out of here and, thank goodness, I won't have to be a – yuk! – *girl* any more.

DAY 7
evening

Wrong! And wrong again!

I gave my five thousand *I must not set fire to the science lab*s to Mr Timmings and he gave me another pile of blank papers. He said that, now, I had to write *I must not blow up the caretaker's bicycle* five thousand times!

Despite my disappointment I couldn't help but admire the girl whose shape I had borrowed.

I went back to my desk, deciding to shape-change into a pen while Mr Timmings wasn't looking. When he noticed the girl was missing, he would go and look for her and I could make my escape.

I stared at my pen and concentrated hard.

I concentrated again.

Nothing happened!

I couldn't do it.

Too many changes in too short a time. I had overloaded my brain-circuits and I was stuck as a *girl*. What would my mates back home say? Me. A *girl*. An *Earth* girl, true, but still a *girl*.

There was nothing for it but to do the work and give the papers to Mr Timmings. Even then, escape was denied me. He insisted on driving me home in his car and handing me over to my (the girl's, that is) parents.

What a journey!

Back home I have experienced many exciting rides. I have visited Andromeda Towers Amusement Park and ridden the Mega Meteorite Run (on real meteorites); I have ridden pillion on Uncle Rom's City Skimmer – minus Uncle Rom, who fell off while swerving to avoid an old-age Arcturian on a Plasma Beam Crossing.

Neither of these comes close to being a passenger in Mr Timmings's Skoda.

For the benefit of any who follow in my tentacle-steps, here is my guide to:

EARTH ROADS
AND HOW TO DRIVE A CAR

1 EARTH ROADS ARE NARROW STRIPS OF CRUMBLY STUFF CONNECTING SOMEWHERE TO SOMEWHERE ELSE. TRAFFIC MOVES ALONG THEM ON WHEELS. SINCE THE WHEELS STAY IN CONTACT WITH THE ROADS (MOST OF THE TIME) INSTEAD OF HOVERING ABOVE THEM AS IS NORMAL, THE ROADS WEAR OUT QUICKLY.

SMALL VEHICLE SPEED 70 MPH

2 ON MANY ROADS, TRAFFIC MOVES IN BOTH DIRECTIONS AT THE SAME TIME AT HIGH SPEED.

3 FASTER VEHICLES ARE PERMITTED TO PASS SLOWER VEHICLES BY MOVING INTO COLLISION COURSE WITH TRAFFIC COMING TOWARDS THEM.

4   (HERE'S THE SCARY BIT.) NOBODY KNOWS WHERE ANYONE ELSE IS GOING OR WHAT ANYBODY ELSE IS DOING OR GOING TO DO. THERE IS NO CENTRAL COMPUTER CONTROLLING THE VEHICLES AND PREVENTING COLLISIONS. EACH DRIVER IS FREE TO DO HIS OR HER OWN THING.

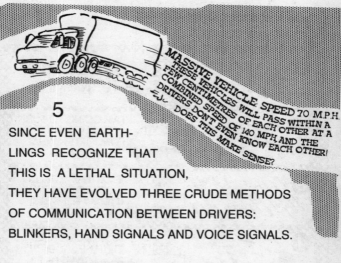

MASSIVE VEHICLE. SPEED 70 M.P.H. THESE VEHICLES WILL PASS WITHIN A FEW CENTIMETRES OF EACH OTHER AT A COMBINED SPEED OF 140 MPH AND THE DRIVERS DON'T EVEN KNOW EACH OTHER! DOES THIS MAKE SENSE?

5
SINCE EVEN EARTH-
LINGS RECOGNIZE THAT
THIS IS A LETHAL SITUATION,
THEY HAVE EVOLVED THREE CRUDE METHODS
OF COMMUNICATION BETWEEN DRIVERS:
BLINKERS, HAND SIGNALS AND VOICE SIGNALS.

BLINKERS (Mr Timmings was very happy to explain this bit to me, though he did seem surprised that it wasn't common knowledge.)

IF A VEHICLE'S **RIGHT** BLINKER FLASHES, IT WILL TURN **RIGHT**.

IF A VEHICLE'S **LEFT** BLINKER FLASHES, IT WILL TURN **LEFT**.

IF A **FEMALE** IS DRIVING, IT MAKES NO DIFFERENCE **WHICH** BLINKER FLASHES – THE VEHICLE MAY TURN **RIGHT**, **LEFT** OR **REVERSE** INTO A **LAMPPOST**. (Mr Timmings had a lot more to say about female drivers, but I'd need another Memory Implant to remember it all.)

HAND SIGNALS

❶ I AM GOING TO TURN RIGHT

❷ I AM GOING TO TURN LEFT BUT I HAVE FORGOTTEN WHAT THE SIGNAL IS

❸ IF YOU THINK I'M OPENING THE WINDOW TO STICK MY HAND OUT IN THIS RAIN YOU'RE BONKERS!

❹ JUST LOOK AT THAT IDIOT! HE SHOULDN'T BE ALLOWED OUT IN A PEDAL CAR!

❺ CENSORED ★★★★★✿!!!!

❻ SORRY, OFFICER, I THOUGHT I WAS ONLY **FIVE** MILES PER HOUR OVER THE SPEED LIMIT

VOICE SIGNALS (often used in conjunction with HAND SIGNALS)

MR TIMMINGS USES THESE MOST OF ALL. THOSE IN MOST COMMON USAGE ARE:

'SUNDAY DRIVERS!'
'MANIAC!'
'DO YOU THINK YOU OWN THE ROAD?'

(WHEN MR TIMMINGS USED THIS LAST ONE, THE OTHER DRIVER ACKNOWLEDGED THAT HE HAD UNDERSTOOD THE QUESTION BY USE OF HAND SIGNAL NUMBER 5.)

SPECIAL NOTE:

SOME DRIVERS HAVE MOBILE TELEPHONES INSTALLED IN THEIR VEHICLES. ACCORDING TO MR TIMMINGS, THESE DRIVERS ARE KNOWN AS POSERS. THE MOBILE TELEPHONE IS NEVER USED TO COMMUNICATE USEFUL INFORMATION, MR TIMMINGS SAYS. ITS SOLE FUNCTION IS TO IMPRESS DRIVERS WHO DON'T HAVE A MOBILE TELEPHONE. (LIKE MR TIMMINGS.)

After what seemed a lifetime (and actually *is* a lifetime if you happen to be a Tropical Gloobial Snowflake Creature), the nightmare trip ended. Mr Timmings stopped the car outside a small house, identical in every detail to the others lining the road.

He took me to the door, which was opened by a female human. A smaller male stood behind her.

'Alicia!' the female cried, hugging me. (Alicia? Yuk!) 'Welcome home.'

Mr Timmings looked puzzled. 'She's only been at school, Mrs Bodkin,' he muttered as he returned to his car, shaking his head.

Mrs Bodkin led me inside. The male, Mr Bodkin, started going on about telling me what was happening, but his wife said, 'No, dear. The child must be exhausted. He – er – she – must go straight to bed. We'll explain in the morning.'

So here I am, in bed. There are three mysteries to be resolved tomorrow:

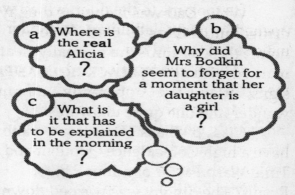

a Where is the **real** Alicia ?

b Why did Mrs Bodkin seem to forget for a moment that her daughter is a girl ?

c What is it that has to be explained in the morning ?

Good night, diary.
Good night, reader.
Tomorrow all will become clear…

DAY 8

…as mud!

It is midday. Soon I shall embark on a journey even more hair-raising than a drive on Earth roads. Better start from the beginning, I suppose. Here are the facts.

Mr and Mrs Bodkin (shape-changed, of course) are my real parents. They arrived on Earth three weeks ago.

How is this possible? you ask. Easy – if you have a family like mine.

While Dad was fixing the dinghy, it drifted into a Class B9 Black Hole. At home, these hazards are normally clearly marked with **SLOW! BLACK HOLE AHEAD** signs, but out here, apparently, you can wander into one quite unawares.

Class B9 Black Holes, as you know, have a high Coincidence Quotient and a Time-Warp Factor of minus 2.77%. Result? The dinghy was warped down to Earth and back in time. It came down only a short distance from the zoo where I landed but, because of the Time-Warp Factor, it got here three weeks before I did.

Mum and Dad had seen the escape capsule leave the caravanette and knew that I would be arriving soon, so they disguised themselves as Mr and Mrs Bodkin while they sorted out a few problems.

The real Mr and Mrs Bodkin and their daughter, Alicia, are in the spare room. Mum used her Hyperion Hypnosis on them. They're quite happy – they think they are a three-piece suite.

Wait a moment! If Alicia has been a small armchair for the last three weeks, how, you ask, did I come to see her when I was being chased by the carnival men? Well, you see, that wasn't the real Alicia. That was – hang on, I think I'd better explain one thing at a time.

Having found somewhere to live, Mum and Dad had three problems:

(a) Finding me, when I arrived on Earth.
(b) Getting back to Earth orbit and the caravanette.
(c) Obtaining hydrogen fuel for the caravanette.

The solutions they came up with were:

(a) Worry about that later. (Hmph!)
(b) A simple matter (Dad says). They have the space dinghy. All that is required is to reverse the polarity of the dinghy's **grossett fluctuation-diverter** and put the

flop-dinget into **cross-bender mode**.

This will cause the **warp-field** of the Class B9 Black Hole to **firtle** a **modulated back-flow wave-pulse** and send the dinghy into orbit. Or, possibly, it won't.

(c) Make the hydrogen.

Amazingly, Dad has actually made the hydrogen – it's stored in the fridge, highly compressed in ten specially adapted vacuum flasks. How did he do it? Read on:

HOW TO MAKE HYDROGEN
(the hard way)

APPARATUS:

THE CONTENTS OF A MEDIUM-SIZED SCHOOL SCIENCE LAB PLUS ONE BICYCLE.

METHOD:

1 DISGUISE YOURSELF AS ALICIA BODKIN AND SNEAK INTO THE LAB.

2 POUR VARIOUS SMELLY SUBSTANCES INTO A HANDY BEAKER AND STIR CAREFULLY.

IMPORTANT! DO NOT LEAVE THAT BOTTLE OF GREEN STUFF NEXT TO THE BUNSEN BURNER.

3 IF DISCOVERED, CLIMB THROUGH WINDOW AND ESCAPE ON BICYCLE.

HOLD IT! DO NOT TAKE THAT BEAKER WITH YOU. IF THOSE CHEMICALS GET SHAKEN ABOUT THEY COULD – OH DEAR, TOO LATE!

4 HIDE REMAINS OF BICYCLE, RETURN TO LAB AND START AGAIN.

RESULT:

TEN FLASKS OF COMPRESSED HYDROGEN.

ONE FURIOUS CARETAKER.
(IT WAS *HIS* BICYCLE.)

ONE BURNT-DOWN SCIENCE LAB.
(YOU REALLY SHOULDN'T HAVE LEFT THAT
BOTTLE OF GREEN STUFF NEXT TO THE
BUNSEN BURNER!)

So, problem (**c**) was solved. Dad
had shape-changed into Alicia, gone to
her school and made the hydrogen. Still
disguised as Alicia (yes, Dad got stuck
for a while, too!) and on the run from Mr
Timmings and the headmaster, he saw
me with my red bucket.

He says he recognized me
instantly – only *I*, he says, could have

shape-changed into something so silly. (He obviously hadn't seen the MAULERS!)

He waved at me, watched me begin to change into Alicia (copying *him*), but then had to run off when he saw the teachers.

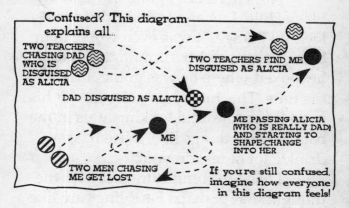

Confused? This diagram explains all...

TWO TEACHERS CHASING DAD WHO IS DISGUISED AS ALICIA

TWO TEACHERS FIND ME DISGUISED AS ALICIA

DAD DISGUISED AS ALICIA

ME

ME PASSING ALICIA (WHO IS REALLY DAD) AND STARTING TO SHAPE-CHANGE INTO HER

TWO MEN CHASING ME GET LOST

If you're still confused, imagine how everyone in this diagram feels!

With problems (**a**) and (**c**) solved, that leaves only problem (**b**).

Dad has been working on that, too. The dinghy is hidden in a lock-up garage a short distance away. We are going there now. According to Dad, he only has a couple more adjustments to make and we shall be off, through the Black Hole and into orbit.

I wish I felt happier about this.

73

DAY 8
later

What a frightening trip!

No. We haven't gone through the Black Hole. I mean the taxi ride to the lock-up garage. It was even worse than being driven by Mr Timmings – at least he looked where he was going, most of the time. This man drove along with his head turned around looking at us in the back, saying things like, 'Nice flasks – drink a lot of tea, do you?'

I tried to comfort myself with the thought that perhaps Earthlings are like the Pod-People of the planet Pookah and have a spare eye in the back of their heads, beneath the hair.

Worse was to come.

When Dad opened up the lock-up garage, the dinghy was –

GONE.

DISAPPEARED.

We're walking home now. My left brain is finishing off this part of the journal while my other two are coming to terms with the fact that we are stranded on this miserable planet.

DAY 9
morning

Hooray! Great news!

No, we haven't found the dinghy, but I can shape-change again.

Bye-bye, Alicia. Can't say it's been nice being you.

Mum and Dad have gone out, leaving me here on the settee – the one in the living-room, not the one that is Mr Bodkin. It has been a relaxing morning, apart from one small incident.

I was reading a book I had found called *Invasion of the Three-headed Lizards from Outer Space* (I like true-life adventures), when the doorbell rang.

I opened the door, forgetting that I was in my own shape, handsome hunk that I am.

The man at the door didn't stop to tell me what he wanted. He dropped his briefcase and shot off down the road like a Kwog-rat with two of its tails on fire.

I have had a quick look in the briefcase. Nothing much in there. Just a few sheets of paper with questions written on them, and this card:

This is to certify that
HORACE DINGBAT
is a genuine
Market Researcher
for
The Peek & Pry Company
and that he is not a cheap confidence trickster

Mum and Dad should be back soon. They've gone to the zoo to see if they can find out where Eric lives. Mum isn't convinced that he is 'one of us', but what else is there to do?

I think I'll watch some of this funny two-dimensional television while I wait for them.

DAY 9
half an hour later

So much for Earth television. I couldn't make head, tail or tentacle of it.

I think it was a film, but the story was really hard to follow. It kept jumping from one place to another for no reason.

It started off with a lot of fighting, lots of guns and things...

Then it changed to a car chase...

Next we saw a big building burning, followed by more fighting, this time with a ball instead of guns...

I suppose the fact that the sound on the television wasn't working didn't help, but, even so…

I've switched off now. I'll read my book until my parents return. I hope the *three-headed lizards* make a better job of things than we're doing.

The people at the zoo have refused to give Eric's address to my parents. I don't think Dad helped by telling them he was Eric's long-lost brother from the planet Bong.

Mum asked what I had been doing while they were out, so I told her about the stupid television programme.

'Fancy that,' Mum said. 'Earthlings still show **THE NEWS** on television.'

She explained that, many years ago on our own planet, we, too, had **THE NEWS**. This made everyone so unhappy that the government banned **THE NEWS** and ordered the Holovision Companies to show only entertainment programmes. Result: everyone was happy again.

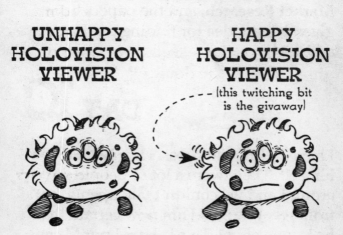

UNHAPPY HOLOVISION VIEWER

HAPPY HOLOVISION VIEWER
- (this twitching bit is the givaway)

Mum thinks the television people on Earth will give up showing **THE NEWS** before long. She says the newspapers here have all but given up *printing* it.

Stur
TURN TO PAGE 5 FOR TODAY'S 'SPOT-THE-NEWS' COMP

I suddenly remembered the man who had come to the door nd showed the papers and card to Mum.

This cheered her up no end. It seems she knows something about **Market Research,** and the papers have given her an idea for finding out Eric's address.

DAY 10

I have it! Eric's address. He gave it to me himself. There were a lot of people around and we couldn't talk openly, but from what he said I am now certain that he is 'one of us'. This is how I put Mum's plan into action.

Early this morning, I shape-changed into Horace Dingbat. Although I had only seen his face for a split second, my Memory Implant had recorded all the details.

Then I set off for the zoo on a bicycle we found in a wooden building in the garden.

While Dad had been at school, disguised as Alicia, he had watched the caretaker riding his bicycle (this was before he blew it up) and was able to give me the following instructions:

HOW
TO RIDE A BICYCLE

1 SIT ON BICYCLE AND GRIP HANDLES WITH HANDS WHILST ROTATING PEDALS WITH FEET.

RIGHT →   WRONG →

YOU SHOULD NOT ATTEMPT TO RIDE A BICYCLE IF YOU POSSESS MORE THAN TWO OF THESE LIMBS

② FALL OFF

③ START AGAIN, OMITTING STEP 2

④ RIDE BICYCLE ALONG THE ROAD, IGNORING ALL OTHER TRAFFIC.
DO NOT BOTHER WITH HAND SIGNALS.
BICYCLES ARE OBVIOUSLY EQUIPPED WITH FORCE-FIELDS WHICH GIVE THEIR RIDERS A SENSE OF TOTAL SECURITY AND COMPLETE INVULNERABILITY.

I left the bicycle at the zoo gates and went in.

The first person I saw was SAVE-THE-WHALES – except that now she was called SAVE-THE-RAIN-FORESTS. I realized at once that she must have married Mr RAIN-FORESTS since we last met.

I went over to ask her where I could find Eric. I was nervous. She wouldn't recognize me in my Horace Dingbat shape, of course, but I couldn't help remembering that the last time I had spoken to her, my part of the conversation had started with 'QUACK'.

No problems this time. She told me that Eric was in the elephant house.

That's where I found him. He was with a big grey animal with its tail on the wrong end.

TAIL, FIXED TO
WRONG END

WHERE TAIL
HAS BEEN
PULLED OFF

So that is why Eric has been sent to Earth. He must be a Special Agent for the GSPCA (The Galactic Society for the Prevention of Cruelty to Animals). His mission, to investigate cases of animal-experimentation on primitive planets.

Our conversation went like this:

MEMORY IMPLANT RETRIEVAL:

GALDATE : 344/67/3388/876 GIVE OR TAKE A DAY

GALTIME: 567/782 I THINK MY WATCH HAS STOPPED

INTERCOSMIC CO-ORDINATES:

X98245.562

Y346639.3002

K77.9935524302 AND A BIT

LOCAL WEATHER: WHO CARES?

<ME>

Good morning, Eric. Horace Dingbat at your service. Peek and Pry Market Research – and I am certainly not a cheap confidence trickster.

<ERIC>

Sorry, mate. No time to talk. I've

been dropped in it good and proper. How on Earth they expect me to clean up this place on my own I don't know.

[PAUSE]

I understood immediately what Eric was *really* saying.

DROPPED IN IT =

LANDED BY DROP-SHIP FROM MOTHER-SHIP IN EARTH ORBIT.

HOW ON EARTH THEY EXPECT ME TO CLEAN UP THIS PLACE ON MY OWN I DON'T KNOW =

I HAVE NOT YET DECIDED WHAT SINGLE-HANDED ACTION I NEED TO TAKE TO PUT AN END TO ANIMAL-EXPERIMENTATION ON THE PLANET EARTH.

From where I stood I could see the elephant clearly. A small piece of tail was still attached to the rear end of the poor creature where it had been yanked off.

I silently wished Eric luck in his lone mission. What a hero! Maybe we could help him in return for helping us.

[CONTINUE]
<ME>

Please, Eric, this won't take long. Answer a few questions and all your problems could be solved.

<ERIC>

Look, mate, you have no idea what my problems are.

<ME>

You'd be surprised.
[PAUSE]

This went on for a while, but, in the end, my personal charm came through and Eric agreed to answer the questions on my sheet of paper.

And what questions! These Market Researchers are nosier than a Silurian Sniffer!

HOW MUCH DO YOU EARN?

WHAT COLOUR UNDERWEAR DO DO YOU PREFER?

WHERE DO YOU LIKE TO GO FOR YOUR HOLIDAYS?

DO YOU PICK YOUR NOSE?

Really! Where I come from it is considered very rude to ask anyone where they like to go for their holidays.

I was relieved to reach the end of the questions and get on to the important part.

[CONTINUE]
<ME>

Now the important part, Eric. In return for your help with our research, your name will be entered in our Prize Draw.

First prize, a Jolly Timeshare Holiday Hut on the island of Vivaespania, just off the Costa Fortune. If you would just give me your address...

[END]

And he did. Eric gave me his address.

I'm on my way back to Mum and Dad now.

Unfortunately I am having to walk.

My bicycle has been stolen.

Thank goodness I have this journal to keep me occupied. There isn't anything else to do, sitting here in this police cell.

Let me explain.

On my way back from the zoo yesterday, I was stopped by a man with a pointed head – well, that was the shape of his hat, anyway.

EARTHLING HEAD SHAPES

Judging from some of the hats I have seen, the heads of Earthlings come in a variety of shapes.

He placed a large hand on my shoulder and said, 'Horace Dingbat, I must ask you to accompany me to the station.'

I explained that I was a stranger in town and that if he needed someone to show him the way to the station he should ask a policeman.

He told me he *was* a policeman.

Good, I thought. They must have found my bicycle. I went along, happily.

At the police station I had to stand in a line of other Earthlings while a little old female Earthling was brought in.

It was an identity parade, like the ones we have on my own planet. You know how it works. A group of victims stands together and the suspect is brought in for them to identify.

Who would have believed that this elderly Earthling could be a hardened criminal – the ringleader, perhaps, of an international gang of bicycle thieves.

'Did she pinch *your* bicycle, too?' I asked the man next to me.

He ignored me, but the old lady didn't. She came right up to me and hit me with her handbag.

'That's him, officer,' she said. 'He came to my house pretending to be a market researcher. While I was making him a cup of tea he stole my life savings from under the carpet.'

I realized then that identity parades are different on Earth.

They threw me into this cell. I wasn't too worried. I was confident I could solve the problem by shape-changing and claiming wrongful arrest.

The trouble is, I can't. I'm stuck again. This time in the shape of the *CHEAP CONFIDENCE TRICKSTER*, Horace Dingbat.

DAY 11
afternoon

Earthlings are food mad! Since I have been here, the policeman has brought me two meals. *Two!* That would keep me going for several months back home.

I suppose I should have realized from the large number of shops I had seen selling cooked foods.

It's quite plain to see that Earthlings

are grazing animals – they have to eat all the time in order to survive.

Food sellers are placed at regular intervals so that there is no chance of starving before reaching the next one. What a way to live!

Anyway, back to my plight.
I have a plan. **Plan X**.

PLAN X

1 PHONE DAD. (I am allowed one phone call.)

2 DAD COMES TO POLICE STATION DISGUISED AS IMPORTANT POLICEMAN. HE SAYS HE HAS COME TO TAKE ME TO HQ.

3 WE ESCAPE!

I have completed Part 1.

I am now waiting for Part 2 and Part 3.

DAY 11
evening

At least I have company in this cell now.
Dad!

Plan X would have worked perfectly, but Dad, as usual, had to overdo things.

He had found a book in the Bodkins' house about the best detective ever. There were pictures in it, too, for Dad to copy.

A short while ago, he burst into the police station wearing a funny hat, smoking an even funnier pipe and carrying a violin case.

'Make way for the great Sherlock Holmes!' Dad bellowed to the policeman at the front desk.

'Bring the prisoner, Horace Dingbat, to me immediately!'

Then he took the violin from its case and began playing a selection of classical favourites.

The violin, I understand, is a musical instrument.

You could have fooled me.

When I heard it, I thought the policeman was torturing someone in the next cell.

So, here we are.

Dad and me.

Prisoners.

The only good thing I have to report is that the policeman has confiscated Dad's violin.

DAY 12

Thank the stars for mums!

My mum in particular.

Guessing things had gone wrong, she set about putting them right – though even *she* had to go over the top. Dad and I were quite surprised when the policeman came and told us the Queen of England was paying a secret surprise visit to the station.

The policeman is a real fan of the Royal Family and he was completely fooled by Mum's shape-change.

She says she threw in a little hypnosis to be on the safe side and was even prepared to use a few tricks she'd learned from watching Galactic Federation Nose Wrestling. Luckily (for the policeman) she didn't need to.

After a quick tour of the police station, the Queen (Mum, I mean) declared a full pardon for all prisoners and told the policeman that she would give us a lift home.

That's the *good* news.

The not-so-good news is that when we got back to the house, I tried shape-changing again. It nearly worked, but not quite. Now I have my own head, but the body of Horace Dingbat.

The *terrible* news is – **THE NEWS.**
The television news, I mean. Dad got the sound working properly and we have just heard.

MEMORY IMPLANT RETRIEVAL:

GALDATE : MALFUNCTION

GALTIME: MILFUNKTION

INTERCOSMIC CO-ORDINATES:

X MILFUNKSHUN

Y FILMANKSHUN

K FULMONKSHUN

LOCAL WEATHER: ISOLATED SANDSTORMS
FOLLOWED BY BRIEF
PERIODS OF FROG-SPAWN.
GENERAL OUTLOOK: BLEAK.

<THE NEWS>

The government has revealed that experts are examining what they believe to be an extra-terrestrial spacecraft discovered in a lock-up garage.

A spokesman for the experts says that the most baffling aspect of the discovery is the technology of the power unit. Although of unbelievably advanced design, it appears to have been taken apart and put back together by a Do-It-Yourself maniac with two left thumbs.

<END>

Mum looked at me.

I looked at Mum.

We both looked at Dad.

Dad began whistling through his right ear-orifice and pretended to count his tentacles.

We have to face it. The dinghy is lost for good. Our only hope now is Eric.

As soon as I recover my shape-change power, I am going to see him.

DAY 14

What happened to **Day 13**? you ask.

Am I avoiding the number **13** because superstitious Earthlings believe it to be unlucky (when all civilized creatures know that the unluckiest number in the universe is **17.37769226625 54354873274688223456673324100908747**)?

Of course not. The truth is that nothing happened. Well, not until late evening, anyway. What happened then depressed me so much that I have put off recording it until now.

I stayed in all day, hoping that my

ability to shape-change completely would come back.

Mum went out on her own. She said she had something important to do but it was a surprise.

When evening came and I still couldn't shape-change properly, we agreed that I should go to Eric's house as I was – my head, Dingbat's body. I wore a wide-brimmed hat, pulled well down.

I went to the house, but Eric wasn't in. Waiting in the street, I passed the time observing the Earthlings.

EARTHLING NOTES

1 Another example of primitive Earth transport. This human uses a large four-legged creature to tow him from place to place.

2 These workers have just dug a hole in the road and then filled it in again.

3 These workers have just dug a hole in the road in exactly the same place as the one which the other workers have just filled in. This phenomenon is common throughout the galaxy and, despite intensive research for zillions of years, no one has ever been able to discover why.

4 This appears to be some kind of
personal flying machine which still
needs a lot of work doing on it.

5 It is good to note that not all of the
higher life forms (those that don't
wear clothes) on planet Earth are
downtrodden. This one has obviously
used its superior intelligence to acquire
for itself a human slave.

It was dark when Eric finally turned up.

He was walking even more unsteadily than most people with only two feet and he was clutching an empty bottle.

I could hear him muttering to himself in a slurry voice. My Memory Implant had packed up, but I think he was saying something like, 'I'm shorry, I'm shorry. I know I shaid I'd never touch another drop, but ish all too mush. Firsht the green shimpon…chumpin…monkey, then the duck an' now the efelum…elephant! Ish not fair…'

I rushed up to him as he reached his door.

'Eric! We have to talk,' I hissed. 'I know who you are and I think you know who I am.'

Eric leaned against the door.

'Shorry, mate. You could be a li'l green man from Venush for all I know,' he said.

'Close,' I said. 'Look.'

I took my hat off, revealing my handsome face in all its glory.

Eric's eyes bulged out and he screamed.

I thought he had begun shape-changing into something more comfortable, but he was just sliding down the door to the ground.

Then, another voice.

'Eric! I've been looking for you everywhere. Where have you been?'

It was SAVE-THE-WHALES...

I mean, RAIN-FORESTS.

Only, no, she'd changed her name *again*. Now she was SAVE-THE-OZONE-LAYER. Amazing! Marriages on Earth seem to last even less time than those on the planet Frogscroople, where the female eats the male immediately after he has signed the life insurance policy.

She knelt down beside Eric. She hadn't even noticed me, so I decided to make myself scarce before she did.

When I got back, Mum and Dad were watching **THE NEWS**.

'And finally,' the man on the television was saying, 'the strange tale of the elephant's trunk...'

We listened.

Someone had been to the zoo, the man said, and taken the elephant's trunk off and stuck it back on its bottom.

A zoo-keeper, Mr Eric Brindley, had been quite upset by the affair and had been reported missing by his girlfriend.

The picture on the television was of SAVE-THE-WHALES-RAIN-FORESTS-OZONE-LAYER. Behind her was the elephant.

'It was me,' Mum confessed after we had switched the television off. 'That was my surprise. I went to the zoo with my mini laser surgery kit and repaired the elephant.'

Dad and I stared at her.

'Well, how was I to know that elephants are *supposed* to have their tails on their face?' she said.

So that is the situation. There hadn't been any animal cruelty at the zoo (at least, not until Mum got involved) and Eric was almost certainly not a secret agent for the GSPCA.

In short, there's no hope.

Not unless we can get the dinghy back from the Earth experts.

DAY 15

We have decided. We resort to Plan Y.

1

WE
GIVE
OURSELVES
UP.

That's it, I'm afraid. The best we can come up with.

The idea is that we agree to show the experts how the dinghy works and then steal it.

The trouble is, giving ourselves up hasn't been so easy.

I was able to shape-change again, so we went to the police station as 'aliens'. Not, I hasten to add, in our own shapes – Dad insisted that we didn't look at all alien in our own shapes and for once I thought he was absolutely right.

So we chose our shapes from a picture on the cover of one of the Bodkins' books.

We found a whole shelf labelled SCIENCE FICTION – DO NOT TOUCH and signed P. BODKIN.

A quick glance showed us that this was the way the Earthlings imagined aliens to be.

'Here's a good one,' Dad cried, pulling a book from the middle of the shelf. 'Really scary – a horrible white shapeless thing with just one big, yellow eye.'

101

HOW-TO-
CRACK-IT BOOKS

WAYS TO FRY AN EGG

by
Sally Monella

A cookery book! It must have been put on the wrong shelf.

Anyway, we eventually found something suitable and set off for the police station.

At the last minute, Mum remembered the Bodkins. She gave them a delayed action command to stop being a three-piece suite some time tomorrow.

They'll be fine, Mum says. No after–effects, apart, perhaps, from a strange desire to wear loose covers and take frequent baths in fabric-conditioner.

At the police station Dad explained that we were aliens and that the extra-terrestrial spacecraft that the experts were studying was ours.

The policeman said, 'Yes, sir,' and called, 'We've got three more here,' over his shoulder to someone in the back.

It appears that since the government announced the discovery of the dinghy, over five thousand people have turned up at police stations all over the country claiming to be the rightful owners.

Special centres have been set up to investigate all the claims and that is where we are now. In a queue.

The man in front of us is wearing a coal-scuttle on his head and claims to be someone called Darth Vader.

DAY 16

Hoards of lizard-scaled Wongolian Moon Warriors with anti-grav packs are descending from the Wongolian mother ship, blasting the frail human beings with their death rays. Whole buildings are being vaporized as flying saucers sweep them with laser canon. Is this the end?

Sadly, no. There are still a hundred and sixty-two pages of this stupid book left – the one we chose our shapes from – and unless we reach the front of the queue soon I might just have to finish it!

DAY 17

We've done it! After the hours of waiting, we finally reached the experts. A couple of shape-changes convinced them we really are aliens. (They suspected sleight of hand when Dad turned himself into a pocket-calculator, but realized he wasn't a real one when two plus two came up as five.)

The clincher came when we turned ourselves back into our real shapes. The experts gasped, and one of them stared at Mum saying that she looked out of this world (his actual words were, *she looks like nothing on Earth*).

The snag is they won't let us near the dinghy. They say we have to spend a couple of years being debriefed (I don't like the sound of *that* at all) and until then we are to be locked away in a secret establishment two miles underground.

Even worse, before we are taken there, we have to attend a WELCOME-TO-OUR-ALIEN-BROTHERS reception with the Prime Minister tomorrow. On the whole I'd rather be back with the Wongolian Moon Warriors.

AN APOLOGY

The publisher and author apologize to the inhabitants of the planet Wongol and its moon. They accept, unconditionally, that these peace-loving razor-fanged people are in no way related to the Wongolian Moon Warriors portrayed in the Earth science fiction book referred to in this journal. They agree, also, that the real Wongolians have never destroyed another planet other than in self-defence or on those rare occasions when they were feeling just a teeny-weeny bit grumpy.

DAY 18

It's been one of those days again.

At least I have been proved right about one thing. We really do have a secret agent here on Earth. Not Eric, though.

At lunch-time today (remember the Earthlings' obsession with food? They even name the parts of the day after it!) we were taken away in a locked vehicle.

The journey to the reception at the Prime Minister's country residence wasn't as bad as my previous trips. Having no windows to look out of helped. We passed the time discussing our situation and agreed that the best thing to do was to go along with everything for the time being and see what turned up.

The reception wasn't too bad. The Prime Minister made a short speech (no more than an hour and a half) welcoming us to Earth and then came over for a chat. He asked us how we liked it here and would we be interested in doing a broad-cast on behalf of his party?

A large table sagged under the weight of piles of food and the other guests confirmed my theory about Earthly eating habits.

EARTH FOOD

Earthlings, I have observed, eat other animals. There were many of these wormlike sausage-creatures at the reception. Imagine their terror, hunted down by humans many times their size before being mercilessly harpooned with miniature wooden spears.

They carried plates of the stuff everywhere they went, sometimes balancing two of them on one arm while they helped themselves to a drink.

Other Earthlings carried more food to the guests on trays. This was, like all those food shops, presumably a precaution against anyone starving to death before they could reach the big table.

After an hour, the Prime Minister announced that he was going to take his honoured guests on a short tour of the house. Two large men with bulges under their jackets wanted to come with us, but the Prime Minister shooed them away.

'No,' he said, 'I shall be quite all right, thank you.'

So saying, he led us out of the room.

The minute the door closed his attitude changed. 'Come on, hurry up,' he said, and led us to a door which opened on to a flight of steps leading down to a basement.

In the basement was a large black vehicle. The Prime Minister bundled us into the back, then got into the driving seat.

Moments later he started the vehicle and we roared up a ramp towards blackness. Then a rectangle of light appeared ahead, expanding as a door opened at the top of the ramp.

VROOOOOOOOOOOOOM!

We burst out into daylight, sped down a narrow drive, crashed through a pair of iron gates and were out on the public road. All this time, the Prime Minister hadn't said a word.

I was pleased about this. At the speed we were going, I wanted him to concentrate on his driving.

He kept looking in the mirror and, turning around, looking through the back window, I could see why. Another vehicle was following us. Switching my vision to Telescopic Mode, I examined the occupants. They were the two men with the bulges.

'Hold on,' the Prime Minister yelled, and wrenched the steering-wheel over savagely.

Our vehicle ripped through a hedge

and, next thing I knew, we were roaring across a field scattering hundreds of white woolly things that, to my astonishment, swore at us in Klongish. (On the planet Klongol, 'BAAA!' is a *very* rude word.)

A glance through the back window showed me that the two men were still on our tail.

CRASH!

We charged through another hedge and across another field.

SMASH!

Through a wooden fence.

OWWWWWW!

(That was Dad. Mum was holding on to him in terror – in a rather painful place!)

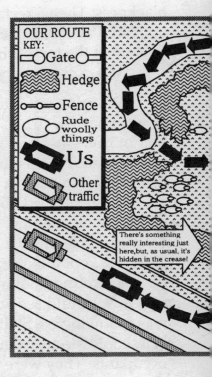

OUR ROUTE
KEY:
Gate
Hedge
Fence
Rude woolly things
Us
Other traffic

There's something really interesting just here, but, as usual, it's hidden in the crease!

116

CRACK!

Through another fence, down a grassy slope and…

SCREECH!

On to a wide road which was divided down the middle.

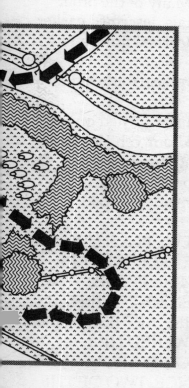

I looked back. We were still being followed. I looked to the front and hurriedly looked back again. I had noticed something rather worrying.

The barrier down the middle of the road separated the traffic into two types. That going in the *same* direction as us and that going in the *opposite* direction to us. The thing that worried me was that *we* were on the side where the traffic was going in the *opposite* direction to us!

The Prime Minister twisted the steering-wheel first one way and then the other, weaving between the vehicles coming towards us. Many of the other drivers used the signals described earlier in this journal, but I learned quite a few new ones too.

Still the other vehicle followed. It was gaining.

The Prime Minister turned on the radio and music filled our vehicle. I was thinking that listening to a nice tune wasn't number one on my list of priorities, when the music stopped.

'HERE IS A NEWS FLASH,' a voice said in capital letters. 'REPORTS ARE COMING IN THAT THE PRIME MINISTER HAS BEEN KIDNAPPED BY THREE ALIENS. THEY ARE BELIEVED TO HAVE OVERPOWERED HIM WHILST BEING SHOWN AROUND HIS COUNTRY RESIDENCE. TWO OF THE PRIME MINISTER'S BODYGUARDS ARE UNDERSTOOD TO BE IN HOT PURSUIT OF THE ESCAPE VEHICLE...'

The Prime Minister switched the radio off and I looked up. All of the traffic had disappeared! Using my Telescopic Vision Mode, I saw why.

In the distance the whole of our side of the road was blocked by vehicles with flashing blue lights. Police!

Up until now there had been no time to consider why the Prime Minister was doing this. Had he gone completely mad, or was this a special treat he dished up for all of his important visitors?

There still wasn't time to consider it. The bodyguards were almost level with us and the roadblock was only a hundred metres ahead.

Instead of slowing down, the Prime Minister increased speed!

The policemen ahead of us took one look and scattered. Unfortunately they left their vehicles where they were. We were right on top of them now...

Twenty-five metres...

Twenty metres...

Fifteen metres...

There was nowhere for us to go, except...

SWERRRRRRVE!

Up the embankment!

I closed my eyes and heard the **CRASH!** as we broke through the fence and then...

Nothing!

Silence.

I braced myself for the jolt of the vehicle thudding back to earth.

Still nothing.

I opened my eyes and looked out.

Still nothing!

Then I looked down.

NO, THIS ISN'T ANOTHER MAP.
THIS WAS THE VIEW FROM MY WINDOW!

Everything was spread out below. The road, the police vehicles; the vehicle which had been chasing us was wedged in the top of a tree with the two bodyguards struggling to climb out.

I realized that they had followed us up the embankment, but that where *they* had returned to earth (almost), *we* had kept going.

We were at five hundred metres and still climbing. One of my brains registered the fact that our vehicle appeared to have grown State of the Art Magnetronic Altarian Thruster Pods.

The Prime Minister turned around to look at us.

'You idiots!' he said. 'You have nearly ruined everything.'

I stared back at him.

At his three eyes: one yellow, one red and one green.

At his tentacles, carelessly draped over the back of his seat.

In all the excitement I hadn't noticed exactly *when* he had shape-changed.

DAY 19

Things are quiet again now. Time, I think, to bring this journal to a close – at least for the moment.

I completed yesterday's entry during the rest of the trip.

I suppose I could describe how the airforce sent jets up to intercept us and how we easily accelerated away from them, but it was all a bit boring after the earlier excitement.

The Prime Minister – who is really one of *us*, of course – eventually brought us down in a secluded part of the countryside and took us to a house that stood all alone.

Inside, he told us everything.

He has been on Earth for quite a while.

He is, in reality, a Special Environmental Agent for the Galactic Organization for Spacewide Health.

GOSH has been keeping an eye on developing planets for a long time, sending in agents, where necessary, to sort them out.

'This planet was in a real mess until I came,' he told us. 'It was no use coming out in the open and telling people they had to start using recycled toilet-paper. They're too stubborn. They'd say, "I'm not having bug-eyed monsters from outer-space telling me how to wipe my bottom!"

'But by impersonating important people – at the moment, the Prime Minister – I have been able to secretly prod them into action to clean up the place.'

When he told us that we had almost wrecked his plans, we protested. What difference would *we* make?

He told us.

'Look,' he said. 'Just as these people are learning the importance of looking after their planet and not wasting their resources, along comes a jolly little family of friendly aliens. The Earthlings learn that, out there, in the rest of the galaxy, there are thousands and thousands of lovely planets.'

'So?' I said.

'So,' he continued, 'the Earthlings say to themselves, "Why bother to look after this planet when there are lots more up there? We'll use this one up and then move on to another!" '

'OK,' I said, conceding the point. 'So what do we do now?'

He explained.

So that is why I am here, with Mum and Dad, back – nearly – where I began.

Nearly, but not quite.

The Prime Minister is back too, after his 'miraculous escape from the wicked aliens'.

He is a real hero, now.

He should have no trouble getting people to do the things he wants them to.

And all the opinion polls agree that if there were an election tomorrow he would win it with a one hundred per cent majority – if not more.

The story of how he saved the planet from the 'wicked aliens' was carried by every major newspaper throughout the world – including *The Daily Messenger*.

THE
DAILY MESSENGER

PRIME MINISTER SAVES THE WORLD

by The Messenger's Political (and Entertainment) Correspondent

Last night the Prime Minister spoke modestly for the first time about his amazing escape from wicked alien invaders.

We now know that these creatures were here on Earth preparing for a full-scale invasion. Only the PM's heroic actions have saved us from a life of slavery under alien dominion.

As reported in yesterday's late editions, the aliens kidnapped the PM from a reception held in their honour, escaping in an alien vehicle which they had somehow managed to secrete in the basement of the PM's house.

Whilst he was their prisoner, the PM learned that the aliens had entered Earth's atmosphere through the hole in the ozone layer.

This had been necessary

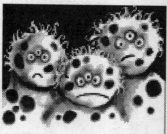

about repairing the ozone layer.

because ozone is poisonous to aliens and dissolves the materials with which they construct their spacecraft.

On hearing this, the PM gave them his speech about the government's Green Policy, including the part

The aliens were so horrified at this news that they dumped the PM in a lay-by and fled back to their own planet, vowing never to return.

At least, that's what the PM told us.

As he says, would he lie?

Meanwhile, the 'wicked aliens', Mum, Dad and myself, are in hiding, waiting for a lift home. Apparently a ship stops by from time to time – could be a year, could be twenty.

We're safe enough here. We weren't given a choice anyway.

And the zoo was very happy with the Prime Minister's gift of three

OUR LATEST FAMILY PORTRAIT

new chimpanzees.

And the *real* Prime Minister? All I know for sure is that he, too, is in a safe place, under hypnosis and heavily disguised.

· Come to think of it, there's definitely something a little odd about the orang-utan in the next cage to us...

END OF JOURNAL
(for the moment)

Editorial Note:

Readers may be interested to learn that Eric left the zoo with his girlfriend, SAVE-THE-WHATEVER, to set up a sanctuary for homeless gerbils in California.

Mr Timmings no longer drives a car. His licence was taken away (for life) after he reversed into a vehicle belonging to a lady magistrate.